POTTS

Edward Potts. Schoolboy on the outside but inside he's Potts, Gunslinger, Vampire Hunter, Master Detective, Oscar-winning Actor, Teenage Idol, Green Hero and . . .

Superpotts – The Masked Avenger!

Is it a bird? Is it a plane? Is it Quasimodo the Hunchback of Notre Dame? No, it's Superpotts, the Masked Avenger, on his way to Right Wrongs and bring Justice to All.

I had been sitting in my Pottscave when the alarm went off: a light shining up in the sky showing a picture of a bird (made with a pair of hands held together so that the thumbs look like its head – nearly as hard to do as the one that looks like a dog's head).

I jumped on to my Pottsmobile (made from three rollerskates and half a bicycle) and rushed off towards the city centre. Within seconds I was in Commissionaire Henderson's office.

'You sent for me, Commissionaire?'

As every passing second was precious, I used my telepathic powers to look into the Commissionaire's brain. There was a small delay before I found it, but at last there it was, a small object the size of a pea going round and round inside his skull . . .

POTTS
by *Jim Eldridge*

Illustrated by
Ann Johns

RED FOX

A Red Fox Book
Published by Arrow Books Ltd
20 Vauxhall Bridge Road, London SW1V 2SA

An imprint of the Random Century Group
London Melbourne Sydney Auckland
Johannesburg and agencies throughout the world

First published by Red Fox 1991

Set in Times
Phototypeset by Input Typesetting Ltd, London

Printed and bound in Great Britain by
Cox & Wyman Ltd, Reading

ISBN 0 09 974560 7

Contents

CHAPTER ONE

Me

MY NAME: Edward Andrew Potts (alias Super-Potts, the Hooded Shadow, Rocky Potts, the Boy Wonder etc etc etc)

MY MISSION: To boldly go where no pupil of Beechwood High School has gone before in saving Planet Earth from its enemies.

MY ENEMIES (and also those of Planet Earth): Miss Fosworth (also known as Chain-Saw Fosworth); Potty Clench, Mad Tompkins of 3C, Mugger Smith, Genghis Khan, Jack the Ripper, Dracula, Spot the dog from next door, Frankenstein, Count Moriarty and Auntie Beryl's killer budgie.

MY FRIEND: Dean Morrison of 2F.

THE OBJECT OF MY SECRET ADORATION: Melanie Winters, the most beautiful girl in the Universe.

MY ADDRESS: 43 Worple Road, Luton, Bedfordshire, England, United Kingdom, Europe, Earth, Near Moon, Milky Way, The Universe, LU6 3HY.

MY SCHOOL: Form 2F, Beechwood High School, Larch Road, Luton Bedfordshire, etc etc etc etc.

MY AGE: 13 years, 4 months, 3 weeks, 2 days, 4 hours, 15 minutes, 37 seconds.

MY PHYSIQUE: Superb.

MY BRAIN: Awe-inspiring.

MY TALENTS: Too numerous to mention.

MY POSITION IN CLASS: 26th.

CHAPTER TWO

SuperPotts – The Masked Avenger

I was walking through the school gates when suddenly . . . CRUNCH!! BIFF!! SMACK!! KICK!! OW!! I was grabbed and brutally maimed by Mugger Smith, the school bully.

I lay there on the ground watching Mugger Smith depart for a full five minutes (just in case he should come back and decide I was not completely dead and then decide to complete the job) before I got up and spat out a nostril. Curses! All that karate training from the book I borrowed from the Library (*Turn YOUR Hands and Feet into Deadly Weapons In Five Minutes* by Fri Sat Sun) was to no avail. Once again Mugger Smith had overcome my superior brainpower and cunning by the simple method of bashing me with a fist the size of a melon.

I was just thinking that, luckily for me, there were no witnesses to my humiliation, when a loud shout from the Pottery Room windows let me know that I was wrong.

'Edward Potts got bashed up again!' yelled a voice. I looked round and there was the whole of the Third and Fourth Years hanging out of the windows and making funny faces at me – including Melanie Winters, the most beautiful girl in the school. Life is just not fair.

I turned to walk off with dignity across the play-ground, but my shoelaces had come undone and I

tripped on them and fell face first on the ground, causing great shouts of mirth and merriment from the Pottery Room windows. This was the Last Straw! I hopped across the playground and into the Boys' Outside Toilets, and once there I changed from Edward Potts, mild mannered and meek schoolboy, into . . .

Superpotts – the Masked Avenger!

Is it a bird? Is it a plane? Is it Quasimodo the Hunchback of Notre Dame? No it's SuperPotts, the Masked Avenger, on his way to Right Wrongs and bring Justice to All.

I had been sitting in my Pottscave when the alarm went off: a light shining up in the sky showing a picture of a bird (made with a pair of hands held together so that the thumbs looked like its head – nearly as hard to do as the one that looks like a dog's head). This was the signal that Big Trouble was happening in the city of Beechwoodville and that help was needed from SuperPotts – the Masked Avenger!

I jumped on to my Pottsmobile (made from three rollerskates and a half a bicycle) and rushed off towards the City Centre. Within seconds I was in Commissionaire Henderson's office.

'You sent for me, Commissionaire?!'

'Yes, SuperPotts. I'm afraid that a new Super-Villain landed here today from the planet Idiot . . . '

As every passing second was precious, I used my telepathic powers to look into the Commission-aire's brain. There was a small delay before I found it, but at last there it was, a small object the size of a pea going round and round inside his skull. I read the Commissionaire's thought.

11

'Gosh!' I said, 'Oh no! The dreaded Mugger Smith has returned to Earth in his Super-Villain guise of the Concrete Brain!'

'That's just what I was going to say!' cried the Commissionaire in astonishment. 'Your powers are truly amazing, SuperPotts. But are they strong enough to take on the Concrete Brain?'

'There is only one way to find out!' I said grimly.

With that I leapt out of his window, intending to fly back to my Pottscave. It was with a Shock Horror realization that I discovered I had forgotten to put on my SuperPotts wings. There was an awful moment as I hurtled towards the pavement six floors below, but just in time I remembered that I was wearing my special underpants with the Levitation Belt. I switched my underpants on and screeched to a halt three centimetres above the ground.

Two minutes later I was back in the Pottscave, working out my plan of action. It was then that my Secret Radio Transmitter crackled into life and the harsh vicious tones of the Concrete Brain cackled out:

'This is a message for the so-called Super-Hero SuperPotts!' he sneered. 'I am taking over this town. From now on I own Beechwoodville and everything in it, and just in case SuperPotts is thinking of trying anything to stop me he'd better think again, because I have a hostage.'

Then came the voice of the woman I love (although she doesn't know it): Melanie Winters.

'Don't let him get away with this, Superpotts. Don't worry about me. The town of Beechwoodville is more important than my life . . . '

Before she could say any more there was the

sound of the Concrete Brain sticking his hand over her mouth and him saying: 'Shut up! OK, citizens of Beechwoodville, you've got my message. From now on your town is *my* town.'

Then the radio went dead.

There was no time to lose I had to act swiftly before the Concrete Brain carried out his threat and took over Beechwoodville. There was no time for me to stand and ponder on the Rights and Wrongs of what I was about to do, no time to think about the Good and the Bad, the Ups and the Downs, the Thoughts of the Great Philosophers . . .

I looked at my SuperPotts watch and got a shock. Good Heavens! I had just spent five precious minutes thinking that there was no time for me to stand and ponder, etc etc. Immediately I picked up my Super Masked Avenger Self-Defence Weapons Kit and set off for the centre of Beechwoodville.

As I flew across Beechwoodville I used my incredible X-ray vision to look through the roofs of buildings in case the Concrete Brain had set a trap for me. Some of the things I saw shocked and astounded me; now I knew what Bensons the Butchers *really* put in their sausages!

Quiet as the night I descended, landing as softly as a snowflake on the roof of Beechwoodville High School. This was where my Super-Villain Radar Tracking Device had told me that the Concrete Brain was hiding out.

I was working my way carefully across the roof when suddenly . . . CRASH THUD!! a lump of concrete crashed through the roof just a centimetre away from me. The Concrete Brain had thrown one of his ears at me! This was my chance! While

he was temporarily deafened I would make my attack!

I saw him lumbering towards me and I leapt at him . . . ! The next second we were both falling off the edge of the roof. Just in time I managed to break free of the Concrete Brain's glue-like grip and soared up into the sky on my huge wings. The Concrete Brain, however, crashed SMACK straight into the playground and broke into a trillion pieces.

The Concrete Brain was no more! At last, the evil Mugger Smith's terrible grip on Beechwoodville High School had been lifted! I landed in the playground and walked across it towards the Main Building, the cheers of the pupils ringing loudly and gratefully in my ears. I opened the doors and stepped in . . .

and a vice-like hand the size of a kilo of bananas grabbed me by the throat.

'And another thing . . . ,' snarled Mugger Smith, 'When I kicked you I bent the toe of my boot.'

And with that he went THUD! and then hung me upside down by my trousers from the Headmaster's door handle, causing me to get a detention.

Curses! I never thought the Concrete Brain would materialize as yet another life form: The Almost-Human Idiot.

CHAPTER THREE

Professor Potts – Doctor

'Right, 2F,' said Mr Whippis, the science teacher. 'I want you to gather round a microscope in groups of four . . . No, *four*, Potts, can't you count, you great idiot . . .' etc etc etc. ' . . . Today we are going to be looking at slides under the microscope. These slides are of sections of skin and human blood and this is exactly the sort of scientific research that all the great physicians of the past did when they were making their discoveries . . . Morrison, take your finger out of your nose or it'll get stuck there . . . Physicians and scientists like Fleming and Jenner and Marie Curie . . .'

* * *

'I think I've identified it, Morrison!'

'What, Professor Potts?'

'This new germ that has baffled all the best brains of the medical profession across the world. I've discovered how it can be destroyed.'

'Professor, you are a genius! Your medical discovery will save the human race from complete destruction!'

'I know.'

Suddenly a nurse rushed in. It was Melanie Winters and my heart was pounding, but I fought back my emotions. I was, after all, a doctor.

'Yes, Nurse Winters,' I said. 'What's the problem?'

'A patient on the operating table has suffered the most terrible relapse and the surgeon who was operating on him, Dr Smith, has fallen over and been taken away drunk. What can we do?' she sobbed. 'There is no other surgeon capable of carrying out this operation in the whole of the Northern hemisphere.'

'What operation is it?' I asked.

'Removing an ingrowing toenail.'

'Surely that's a simple operation,' said Morrison.

Nurse Winters shook her head. 'This operation is to remove it from his *brain*.'

'Ugh!' said Morrison, and fainted.

I took Nurse Winters in my arms and looked deep into her eyes. 'Leave it to me,' I said.

'You mean . . . you can do it?' she asked, a light of hope in her eyes.

'Of course,' I said. 'After all . . . I am a doctor.'

'But no one has ever done this operation before!' blurted out Morrison, who had now come to. 'And the brain is such a delicate organ.'

'I know,' I said. 'I have one of my own.'

With that I followed Nurse Winters to the operating theatre.

The patient was laid out on the operating table. Good heavens! it was Mr Clench (also known as 'Potty' Clench), the drama teacher at Beechwood High School! I never knew he had a brain, let alone a toenail growing inside it!

'Stand back!' I told everyone. 'Let me through.'

A buzz of excitement went around the operating theatre. 'It's Professor Potts, the genius of medicine who has so far discovered four hundred and eighty-three new diseases, at least three hundred and ninety-seven of which have been named after him,

17

including Potts' Knee, Potts' Elbow, Potts' Nose and Potts' Cough.'

I stepped up to the operating table.

'Scalpel . . . '

'Scalpel.'

'Forceps . . . '

'Forceps.'

'Funny curly things with metal handles . . . '

'Funny curly things with metal handles.'

After a few sharp cuts with my trusty Swiss penknife (complete with corkscrew and funny hooked thing for taking stones out of horse's hooves) I laid bare the patient's brain. I spotted the toenail, embedded between the bit for thinking about maths and the bit for thinking about watching television.

'Just a few seconds more . . . ' I said.

Then, with a quick tug, I removed the malignant ingrowing toenail and sewed up Mr Clench's head with a few skilful stitches, signing my name at the end with a bit of fancy embroidery.

'There,' I said. 'He should be ready to start thinking again after half an hour's rest.'

I let Nurse Winters mop my brow, more to please her than because I had worked up a sweat, and then left the operating the theatre to rapturous applause, stopping only to sign a couple of autographs for two admiring surgeons.

* * *

Later, in my surgery in Harley Street I was feeling unhappy. All right, I was a rich and famous doctor, but was that enough to satisfy me? How could I ever really be happy while the human race is still racked by such dreadful diseases as spots, dandruff and bad breath? I would not be able to rest until

all the world's diseases and germs had been eliminated for ever.

I picked up my microscope and took a quick look, checking to see if any new and unidentifiable germs had appeared on Earth in the last few minutes. And, sure enough, there was one!

I sucked in a deep breath of horror, for this was not just any ordinary old germ. This was a Monster Germ which glared back at me up the microscope with a look of evil and triumph as if to say, 'Do your worst, Doc! There ain't nothin' you can do can destroy *me*!'

Oh no?! Eat your heart out, sucker! I thought.

I rushed for my medicine cabinet and started to make a concoction from all the medicines at my disposal: indigestion tablets, sun-tan lotion, toothpaste with different coloured stripes . . . everything known to medical science. A few minutes later I had the mixture bubbling away over a burner. As I watched it froth and bubble, like the thickest kind of soup, I knew that this medical potion was the only thing that stood between this Monster Germ and the destruction of the human race as we know it. Even as I brought the stuff to the boil and added a pinch of salt, I could see that the Monster Germ was already prising itself free from the microscope and slurping its way across the top of my laboratory desk towards me, determined to use me to spread this terrible infection and plague and things.

Just as the Germ was about to pounce, my antidote mixture came to the boil, I snatched it off the burner and hurled it at the Monster Germ.

The Monster Germ reeled back in horror, chucking bacteria and viruses and microbes at me, but it was too late . . . ! My antidote splashed it and with a squeal the Monster Germ curdled and turned into a little spot of harmless grease. I had done it! My mastery of medicine had saved Planet Earth from a new and deadly disease!

* * *

'Your turn, Potts,' said Mr Whippis, and he thrust me towards the microscope. I peered down through the eyehole and saw something wriggling about at the other end.

'This is a section of human blood,' said Mr Whippis. 'That is a white corpuscle . . . '

I did not hear the rest of his words because the next second everything went black and I thudded to the floor.

'Some people,' I dimly heard Mr Whippis tell the rest of the class, 'just cannot stand the sight of blood.'

CHAPTER FOUR

Potts in Love

I was standing in the corridor outside our classroom (I had been sent there by Miss Fosworth for making a Rude Noise In Class – a charge of which I was completely innocent – and I was even now composing in my head a letter which I planned to send to the Court of Human Rights in Strasbourg: 'Dear Sir or Madam, I am writing to you to bring to your attention a situation of such injustice that the world will quake in its shoes . . . etc etc etc') when two girls walked past: one of them Linda Tompkins – known in the school as Mad Tompkins of Class 3C – and a vision of such loveliness that it was a wonder that birds did not break out into song on the spot. It was Melanie Winters herself. For years I had been too tongue-tied even to smile at her, let alone reveal to her my secret love for her. As our paths rarely crossed, the chances of her ever finding out how I felt were on a level with Brighton Football Club winning the World Cup. Yet here she was, only a few paces away from me! All I had to do was step forward and say 'Melanie Winters, I adore you! Let me crush you in my arms and take you away from all this!' I took a deep breath and as the dream-like Melanie and the nightmarish Mad Tompkins drew level with me, apparently deeply involved in dismembering a piece of bubble gum, I spoke.

'Aa . . . ' I croaked.

Melanie and Mad Tompkins looked at me with puzzled looks on their faces.

'Aa . . . ' I croaked again.

The two girls backed away from me and continued on their way down the corridor.

'Who was that?' asked Melanie.

'Potts of 2F,' said Mad Tompkins. 'He's an idiot.'

'He sounds like a parrot,' said Melanie.

My heart sank. Why did it have to be like this?! Why could I not reveal the depths of my feelings! I let out a groan born of the anguish and pain of love. Almost immediately, the door of the classroom was wrenched open and Miss Fosworth glared out at me.

'If I hear you making any more of those funny noises I shall report you to Mr Henderson!'

'But . . . ' I began.

It was no use. She slammed the door shut just as I poked my head into the classroom to explain my defence. I reeled back against the opposite wall of the corridor, clutching my nose and thinking: curses, thanks to Miss Fosworth's brutality now my nose will swell up and the next time I see Melanie Winters it will look like I'm wearing a ripe tomato where my nose ought to be. Oh, agony! It was never this impossible in films or stories . . .

* * *

'Oh, Lancelot! How handsome you look in that suit of armour!'

'Thank you, my Queen. I only got it back from the cleaners this morning and I thought I'd wear it especially for you. Unfortunately, there are still one or two dents in it from where they've ironed it . . . '

'That does not matter. All that matters is that you are here with me. Shall we take a stroll around the grounds?'

'In faith, yea. Beechwood Castle is so lovely at this time of year.'

With that we set off, me clanking along behind this vision of loveliness and beauty. From a window above us a minstrel started singing a song of praise:

'Oh fair, lovely Queen Melanie Winters,
I can't think of anything to rhyme with it but
Polo Minters . . .'

'Shut up!' I said to the minstrel, with a light smile, and chucked a rock at him, bashing him on the nose so that he disappeared back inside the castle.

'Oh, Lancelot, you are so manly,' sighed the Queen.

'I know, my lady,' I said, 'but beneath this manly chest beats a heart that has a secret.'

'A secret?'

'Yes, and this secret is my love for . . .'

The next second there was a CLANK and a CLONK as King Dean Arthur Morrison appeared.

'Ah!' he said, 'Why, it is my best friend Sir Lancelot Potts and my dear wife, Queen Guinevere Winters, the two people I care for most in the whole wide world. How nice to see you two taking a stroll around the castle on this fine bright day.'

'Hush, dear,' said Guinevere. 'Lancelot was about to tell me a secret.'

'A secret?' said King Dean Arthur.

'Yes,' said Lady Guinevere. 'It is about a love he has for . . . For who, Sir Lancelot?'

'For Bassett's liquorice allsorts,' I said with a

gulp. 'I love the taste of the ones with little blue bobbles on.'

'Why, then!' said King Dean Arthur. 'I shall order a ton for you. Come, let us all go and take a quick swim in the moat. First, I suggest we take our armour off, otherwise it will go all rusty.'

See? I know exactly how Sir Lancelot felt. Not that Dean Morrison would ever get Melanie Winters to go out with him and be his girlfriend, Morrison would be lucky to get anything even human to go out with him, and I say this even though he is my best friend.

No, there is only one answer and that is to adopt the Direct Approach that you see in some of these films on TV . . .

* * *

Hot Love In Tough Town

As soon as I walked into Beechwood School dining hall and first set eyes on her I knew she was for me. Melanie Winters, the beauty of 3C. There was no time for hesitation. I walked straight across the dining hall up to the counter where she was choosing her dinner.

'Melanie Winters,' I said.

She gave me a look. I could see in her eyes she was thinking, 'Who is this handsome guy and what does he want with me?'

'Yes?' she said. 'Who are you?'

'Ed Potts, 2F,' I said. 'And you're the girl for me.'

With that I took her in my arms, crushed her to me and poured burning kisses on her lips. Then I stepped back.

'There!' I said. 'What do you say?'

'I'll tell you what I say,' she said. 'Do that again and I'll sue you for assault, sexual harrassment, and personal invasion. Till then, eat this, sucker!'

And with that she went BOP! and smacked me in the mouth with her dinner tray.

'Gnnngggg,' I said as I walked back to my table, her tray sticking out of my mouth.

CHAPTER FIVE

Two-Gun Potts – Gunslinger

I was walking out of the school gates on my way home after school. Behind me I could hear the voice of Melanie Winters as she chatted to her hideous best friend, Mad Tompkins. My heart beat faster, about a hundred thousand revs per minute. Oh, I thought, if only something could happen right now that would show me in a wonderful light, so that she could see me as a hero! If only a pram was to head out of control towards the road so that I could make a dive for it and grab it before it gets crushed by a passing car, and then Melanie would rush up to me and say, 'Oh, Edward! You are my hero!'

Perhaps, I thought, a thunderbolt of lightning could suddenly fall out of the sky and strike Mad Tompkins, and I could rush to save the life of Melanie's best friend and she would be grateful to me for ever. (The trouble is, that sort of thing seems to require giving the injured party the kiss of life, and to be honest I'd rather kiss next door's dog.)

Just at that moment the chance for me to show myself as a hero in front of Melanie arose: Mugger Smith suddenly stepped away from the wall he was holding up and stood right in my path.

'Right, Potts.' he said. 'Give me fifty pence.'

I hesitated. What should I do? Hand him over the fifty pence and reveal myself as a coward and a weakling and a failure in the eyes of Melanie; or stand up to him and show her that I am a hero? I made my decision.

'NO!' I said loudly, and then I added in a whisper, so that only Mugger Smith could hear, 'I'm afraid I haven't got any money.'

Behind me I could hear the two girls waiting to see what would happen. Mugger Smith glared at me.

'Haven't got it?!' he snarled, his brain having to work overtime to grasp this concept. 'Then get it!'

And with that, BASH THUMP BIFF THUD!! and I was left sitting on the pavement counting my teeth, while Melanie and Mad Tompkins stepped over me to go home.

Curses! I thought. All Mugger Smith has to his advantage is his huge size: built like a brick wall on legs. If we were in another time and place, things would be different . . .

* * *

Dodge City. I rode into town on my faithful old horse, Jeremiah, and took stock of the place. Here and there gunslingers were shooting each other. I rode past the Sheriff's office and noticed that it had long since been boarded up. There was no Law in this town.

I pulled up outside the Swinging Bat Saloon, hitched Jeremiah to the hitching rail, and strolled on in to the Saloon. Inside there was the sound of someone playing the piano. Why, it was old One-Finger Barnstaple! former music teacher of Beechwood Gulch, playing as badly as ever.

I pushed my way through the crowds to get to the bar.

'Yup?' said the bartender. 'What'll it be?'

'Give me a cola,' I snarled.

'One cola coming up.'

As the bartender poured it out for me he said: 'You're new in town here, ain't you, stranger?'

'I sure am,' I said. 'And I'm looking fer someone.'

'Who might that be?' asked the bartender.

I lifted up my glass.

'I'm looking fer Mugger Smith.'

At that there was a sharp intake of breath from everyone in the Saloon. An awful silence hung over the place.

'Did you say . . . Mugger Smith?!' asked one of the dancing girls, her eyes wide in fear.

'Sure did,' I said. 'And who might you be, pretty dancing girl?'

'They call me Winters,' she said. 'Melanie Winters. But listen, stranger, you don't want to tangle with Mugger Smith. He's big and he's mean and he's ornery.'

'It don't matter how big a man is when he's up against . . . Two-Gun Potts.'

Again there was a mass gasp from the people in the Saloon, and then the word went round like a buzz.

'It's Two-Gun Potts! Two-Gun Potts is in town!'

I put down the glass.

'Pass on the word to Mugger Smith,' I told the bartender. 'Tell him I'll be out on the Main Street waiting for him.'

'When shall I tell him you'll be there?' asked the bartender, quivering slightly in fear.

'Tell him to make it . . . High Noon,' I said.

With that I tossed my empty glass towards the

bartender and strolled back out to the Main Street. As the digital watch hadn't been invented yet, I used the sun to check the time. Two and a half minutes to ten. I was just wondering what to do for the next couple of hours when a kid came rushing towards me, looking agitated.

'Help! Help!' he yelled. 'Rustlers!'

'Where?' I asked, at the same time whistling for my faithful horse Jeremiah.

'Out at our ranch, the Bar-B-Q!' said the kid. 'They're stealing our herd!'

I wondered what sort of cattle the kid had: long horns; short horns; horns that go beep-beep?

'Herd of what?' I asked him.

'Herd of chickens,' he said.

'Of course I've heard of chickens,' I snarled, geting annoyed. 'But I'm talking about cows.'

'No, no,' said the kid. 'A chicken herd!'

'So what if a chicken heard, I've got no secrets from chickens.'

'You don't understand,' said the kid. 'They're rustling our chickens!'

Suddenly I realized what was happening! Chicken-rustlers, the worst rustlers of all! (Well, almost the worst. *The* worst are the people who rustle crisp packets at the pictures during the good bits.)

'Okay, kid!' I yelled. 'Let's go!'

We thundered out of town, a dust cloud stirring up behind us, heading for the Bar-B-Q Ranch. Through Death Valley we galloped, down and then up both sides of the Grand Canyon, over the Rocky Mountains and across the Mexican Desert until we reached the Bar-B-Q Ranch. We were just in time! The rustlers had been trying to round up the chickens, but one ornery old chicken called Chicken

33

Licken had realized what was going on and had persuaded the other chickens to stampede. Now thousands of chickens were charging around the ranch stirring up clouds of dust as the rustlers fought to bring them under control. It was at this point that the kid 'n me galloped in.

'Okay!' I yelled. 'You're all under arrest!'

And with that I pulled my six-guns from my holsters (three in each hand) and pointed them at the rustlers.

It was only then that I recognized them. It was the dreaded James Gang, made up of three fierce brothers: Strawberry James, Raspberry James, Blackcurrant James, and their mother Mama Lade. (Their family name used to be 'Jams' but their grandfather, Jim Jams, changed it because he got fed up with everyone calling him 'pyjamas'.)

'It's only one guy and a kid!' sneered Strawberry James. 'They can't do nothing to us! Shoot 'em down!'

With that they all went for their guns.

PING!

I fired just one bullet, but that was all it needed. That one bullet knocked the gun out of Strawberry James's hand, and then ricocheted around the ranch, knocking the guns out of the hands of the rest of the gang.

'Okay,' I said to the kid. 'Tie 'em up. We're taking 'em back to town. There's a reward for each of these hombres, enough to feed you 'n your ma 'n pa 'n brothers 'n sisters 'n all these chickens for ever.'

'Wow!' said the kid. 'You must be the bravest and toughest cowboy who ever lived.'

'Guess I am,' I said modestly, 'but that's the way it is. By the way, son, what's your name?'

'Twerp,' said the kid. 'Wire Twerp, and when I grow up I want to be a marshal.'

'If that's what you want to do then that's what you will do,' I said. 'Coz always remember this – a man's gotta do what a man's gotta do. Now, if you'll all excuse me, I got important business back in Dodge City.'

And with that I shook hands with the kid and all his family, gave Chicken Licken a friendly pat on the beak, and then rode off into the sunset towards Dodge City.

I checked the time by the sun. Half past eleven. I had plenty of time.

When I reached Dodge City it was noon. High Noon. High Noon in Dodge City, and Noons don't come any higher.

The Main Street was deserted, except for me, waiting. Even my faithful horse Jeremiah had sought refuge in the Saloon.

The whole town was hushed, waiting. Suddenly, from down the other end of the street came the thud of enormous feet and the jangle of spurs . . . and then there he was! Mugger Smith, with so many guns hanging on him he looked like a walking gun shop. He had a gun on each hip, three more round the back, two shotguns under one arm, and a Uzi sub-machine gun under the other.

'I hear you're looking fer me, Two-Gun Potts!' he called.

'I sure am, Mugger Smith,' I called back. 'And you know why I'm here.'

'I sure do,' called back Mugger Smith. 'So go on: draw!'

36

Before his hands could even touch his guns, my fingers had snatched my Colt 45s at incredible speed from their holsters and PAM PAM PAM PAM PAM PAM PAM PAM!!!! in a hail of bullets I had cut off his gun belt. He stood there with all his guns lying in the dust around him. I levelled my guns at him, cocked back the hammer, and Smith started to shiver. Then he fell to his knees.

'Don't shoot me!' he begged. 'I'm too young to die!'

I paused, thinking it over. What the hell, Two-Gun Potts had never shot an unarmed man yet. I twirled the guns around in my hands, and then thrust them back in my holsters.

'See that you change your ways from now on, Smith,' I said, and with that I turned and headed off down the Main Street, into the sunset.

* * *

Suddenly CLONK! a brick hit me on the back of the head and I crashed face down into the dust. I rolled over and looked up, and saw Smith walking away from me. His last words shattered the stillness of the afternoon.

'See that you bring in fifty pence tomorrow!'

CHAPTER SIX

Edward Potts – Mountaineer

I was sitting at the kitchen table, my eyes on the
back of Dad's head, trying to read his brain and
see if there is any truth in telepathy, and whether
I was, in fact, telepathic. I was having a great deal
of difficulty in achieving this: I closed my eyes but
all I could see was darkness and the inside of my
eyelids. It occurred to me that the reason for this
is that Dad hasn't got a brain worth reading. Either
that or he was too tough a subject, his brain being
protected by many centimetres of bone in the form
of his skull. Also his hair is very greasy, which may
have been interfering with my astral thought waves.
Maybe I should have started with someone – or
something – easier. I wondered if our cat had got
any good thoughts?

I was just scouring the kitchen for the cat, when
Dad suddenly said:

'Edward, can you go to the cellar and see if you
can find the small pliers. My glasses have come
apart.'

Wow! Dad spoke to me, just after I was thinking
about him! Was that a sign that I really am a Tele-
path? I tried to tune in to his thoughts. Actually it
was easier than I expected, mainly because he was
saying them aloud to me. They were as follows:

'The pliers I mean are the small ones with the
blue handle and they are on the top shelf on the
wall where I keep the tools.'

'No problem,' I said, and off I went to carry out the task. Just before I went, I asked him: 'Dad, do you think I'm telepathic?'

He didn't answer; just gave me a strange look. I guess he was too stunned at the thought that a child of his may be capable of telepathy. As I went down the stairs to the cellar I thought I heard him mutter something. It sounded like 'The boy's finally going round the bend!' – although as I *was* actually going down the stairs I suppose I must have misheard him.

Once in the cellar I began the search for The Small Pliers With The Blue Handles – the top shelf, Dad had said – and then I froze.

The top shelf! All right, most cellars are so tiny you bump your head even if you're walking around bent over double like you've got your nostrils caught in your shoelaces, but *our* cellar has got this enormous high ceiling, and the top shelf looked pretty high up the wall to me.

I considered going back upstairs and telling Dad I couldn't find the pliers, but I knew this would just lead to a major interrogation of 'are you sure you looked properly?' and 'if I want anything done in this house I have to do it myself' and 'maybe you'd do more to help if you had less pocket money' and so on and so on, etc etc etc.

I stood at the bottom of the wall and tried to work out how best to get to the top shelf. There was a chair, but as two of its legs were broken it didn't seem like a good idea to use it. There was only one way up: I would have to climb up from shelf to shelf.

I looked at the wall in front of me, reached up, and began my climb . . .

OCTOBER 15th:

Here we are at Base Camp on Mount Everest. I have a dozen Sherpas to help me, and loads of ropes and metal things with hooks on, so I am all ready to go. The weather looks as if it could blow up a bit of a storm, but we go tomorrow at first light.

OCTOBER 17th:

Five thousand feet. Two days up the mountain and a blizzard blew up last night. Half the Sherpas packed up and went home because they said the blizzard was the worst they had ever seen on Everest and they reckoned it was impossible to go on. I know I can conquer this mountain.

OCTOBER 20th:

Ten thousand feet. Temperature at minus ten degrees. Blizzard and general weather conditions getting worse. I can tell this because of the amount of interference on my portable TV set which has prevented me from watching *Blue Peter*, which was supposed to have an item about my climb. Another three Sherpas packed up and went back down the mountain again this morning, claiming that this climb is too dangerous. I am faced with one problem: because of the constant wet weather all my ropes have shrunk, as have my clothes. I am being strangled by my shrinking trousers.

OCTOBER 22nd:

Fifteen thousand feet. Temperature twenty degrees below freezing. Constant downpour of freezing rain, hailstones and snow. Cannot see more than a centimetre in front of my face. Teeth frozen. Today the last of the remaining Sherpas told me they have decided to pack it in. I shall be sorry to see them go, particularly because it means there is no one left to play Trivial Pursuit with me.

OCTOBER 26th:

Twenty thousand feet. Weather getting worse. Hurricane another problem to add to the snow, freezing rain, blinding snowstorms and hail. Today I passed a Yeti as I was climbing up. I stopped and put up the tent and we had a game of Trivial Pursuit together. The Yeti made strange gurgling sounds at me. When I translated them with my instant Translator Computer I found that it was telling me this is the worst weather the Yetis have ever known on Everest and he is packing up and going back down the mountain to the valley below until the weather improves. I shall continue with my climb.

OCTOBER 27th:

Zero feet. Avalanche came down the mountain last night and took me back to the bottom. Weather worsening. I shall not be defeated. I shall start again tomorrow.

NOVEMBER 1st:

Ten thousand feet. Temperature forty degrees below freezing. Managed to sprint a bit the last few days. This was because I lost a lot of equipment during the avalanche, so I can travel

lighter. This will be the first ever Solo Conquest of this giant mountain.

NOVEMBER 5th:

Fifteen thousand feet. Firework Night. Tried to light some fireworks but the blizzard blew them out. Had to make do with sparklers instead. So cold today that when I put the tent up it froze into a block of ice and broke into a million pieces as I tried to get inside it. It doesn't matter; nothing will stop me getting to the top of this mountain.

NOVEMBER 7th:

Twenty-three thousand feet. Temperature minus sixty degrees. Thermometer frozen solid, so it could be colder. All my equipment fell to bottom of mountain in another avalanche, so am climbing up using only hands and feet.

NOVEMBER 9th:

Twenty-six thousand feet. Temperature ninety degrees below freezing. I believe I am nearly at the top, but visibility is so bad that I cannot see more than one thousandth of an inch in front of me, and when I breathe out my breath turns into solid chunks and mists up my glasses.

NOVEMBER 12th:

Twenty-nine thousand feet, and I have only just remembered that Everest is only twenty-seven thousand feet high, so where am I? With a shock I realize that I am not on Everest at all, I am even higher than the world's highest mountain . . . I have reached the top shelf of the Potts's cellar!

My frozen hands reach out and with one I place the Union Jack firmly in the ice-pack, while with the other I stretch and just manage to grasp a pair of small pliers with blue handles . . .

'Here you are, Dad. The pliers.'

'*There* you are! What took you so long? You've been away long enough to have been up Everest and back.'

He settled down to mend his glasses and behind his back I allowed myself a little chuckle. Little did he know . . .

CHAPTER SEVEN

Rocky Potts and The Case of the Missing Rubber

'Where is my rubber pots?!'

I looked up from what I was doing (which was inventing a plastic nose so that you can walk around on the planet Pluto without having to wear a space helmet) and saw Miss Fosworth glaring at me.

I turned around and looked at Goofy Biggins, who sits behind me in History, in case she was talking to him, but he had his head down. I turned round and looked at Miss Fosworth, who was still glaring at me. When adults look at me like this my ears go red, which makes them think I've done something I shouldn't.

'Where is my rubber pots?' she growled again.

It occurred to me that her grammar was all wrong; she should have said: 'Where *are* my rubber pots?'

I was just about to correct her on this point, when it crossed my mind that it was very odd that she should have lost a whole lot of pots, and especially rubber ones. And just what do you use a rubber pot for? For planting a rubber plant in, I suppose?

I was just opening my mouth to ask her where she had last seen these pots, when it dawned on me that what she was really asking was:

'Where is my rubber, Potts?'

Just in time, I closed my mouth again and gave her a friendly smile.

It did not work.

'What are you laughing at?!' she bellowed. 'Do you think it funny that I've lost my rubber?! Is it a matter of some hilarity and amusement to you that some person in this class has seen fit . . .' etc etc etc.

After about ten hours of a huge lecture on what is and what is not funny, she turned to the rest of the class and demanded:

'Who had my rubber last?'

At which, they all pointed at me and said:

'Potts!'

'No I did not!' I called back, to which Miss Fosworth snapped:

'Silence! Potts, you will stay behind at break and look for it!'

Huh! Framed! There is no justice in this world! Where was the Righter of Wrongs who would leap in and solve the mystery of the missing rubber and so save my reputation . . . ?

* * *

We were in the rooms of that detective genius, Sherlock Potts, at 220b Bacon Street. The Great Detective (me) was standing looking out of the window, a Great Thought hovering over his head.

'Hand me that violin, Morrison,' he said to his faithful friend.

'Gosh, Potts, are you going to play it while you Solve a Mysterious Clue concerned with the Case of the Missing Rubber?'

'No,' I said, 'I am going to pick my nose with the curly bit at the end.'

Actually, nowadays it is unlikely tha great detectives would play the violin; they're more likely to play the electric guitar or keyboard. However, it doesn't have the same feel to it. I can just imagine it: 'Hand me that electric guitar, Watson. While I ponder the Strange Case of Riding a Bicycle Without Lights, I wish to play the Greatest Hits of the Eurythmics.' Then KERANgggggggg BASH dadadadadaADADADADA brrrmmmm twanggggggg!!!! until the Riot Squad arrive and nick you for making a noise.

Also, modern detectives don't act like Sherlock Holmes. Instead of saying things like 'Elementary!' and "Pon my soul!' and stuff, they drive around in superfast cars and kick in doors and shout 'Freeze!' and 'Make my day, sleazeball!'

They also have TOUGH names like Dirty Harry, Filthy Robert, Iron Man Mike, etc. A modern detective presented with the Case of the Missing Rubber wouldn't hang about playing musical instruments; he'd be in there, kicking in doors and bashing people . . .

* * *

Anyway, I was sitting in my office, practising karate chops on my desk to toughen my hands, when my door opened and a scrawny little guy stumbled in.

'Rocky Potts, Private Detective?' he asked in a frightened sort of voice.

'That's what it says on the door,' I snapped, and I popped another sweet in my mouth. A hard lemon drop that tasted of real lemons. That's coz I'm tough. No one messes with Rocky Potts.

'You've got to help me,' he begged. 'There's been a terrible tragedy!'

50

'Life is a tragedy,' I told him. 'Life is tough. Life is mean. The weak go to the wall and down the tubes till they reach the sewer. The tough stay on top. It's a mean, mean world and down those mean streets it gets meaner.'

I kicked my desk in half, breaking my big toe in the process, but that's coz I'm tough.

'Spill it,' I said. 'Who are you and why are you here?'

The little guy threw a scared look over his shoulder. It hit the wall behind him, bounced off and smacked him in the back of the head.

'Ouch!' he said.

'Just get on with the story,' I snarled.

'My name is irrelevant . . . ' he began.

'Mr Irrelevant,' I snarled, writing it down. 'Is that with one "r" and two "l"s, or two "r"s and one "l"?'

'I mean, it doesn't matter,' he said, his face looking more nervous by the second.

'It may not matter to you,' I said, 'but good spelling is important to a Private Investigator.'

'I mean my name is irrelevant,' he said. 'Actually it's Henderson.'

'So!' I snarled. 'Using an alias, huh? Okay, Henderson or Irrelevant or whatever your name is, what's the problem?'

He gulped, then began to spill the bad news.

'I'm the Headmaster of Beechwood High School,' he began.

I sucked in my breath and nearly choked on my lemon drop.

'Beechwood High! That hell-hole! Of all the dumps in all the world . . . !'

'I know,' groaned Henderson or Irrelevant.

'Let me guess, you want me to go there and put down a riot?'

He shook his head.

'No,' he said. 'I want you to find a rubber.'

I thought over what he had just told me.

'Uh-huh,' I said. 'This rubber's missing, right?'

'Right,' he nodded.

'Okay,' I said. 'My rates are fifty pence a day plus all the bullets I need. But first I need some details. For a start, have you got a picture of this missing rubber?'

He pushed a grubby photograph across the desk to me. It was a picture of a pen and pencil set. The rubber in the picture looked like nothing special, just an ordinary sort of rubber, the kind you'd pass in the street and not notice.

'Any distinguishing features on it? EP 4 MW, that kinda thing?'

He shook his head. This guy didn't know much. I shoved another lemon drop in my mouth and sucked.

'Where was this rubber seen last?' I asked.

'It was in Miss Fosworth's classroom . . . '

I nearly choked on my lemon drop.

'Not Chain-Saw Fosworth?!' I gasped. 'Choppd up a whole class in '89 and sold 'em as sausages?!'

He blanched.

'No . . . ' he began.

'Don't tell me "No"!' I snarled. 'I know when I'm being set up!'

With that I jumped him before he could move and tied him to a chair with his shoelaces and a string from a conker. OK, he may've been telling the truth, but I was taking no chances.

Ten minutes later I was creeping along a corridor

at Beechwood High. In one hand I held a .38 combined automatic sub-machine gun; in the other I balanced a weapons launcher with a heat-seeking missile.

I reached the door marked '2F' and peered in. There she was. There was no mistaking that cruel smile on that tough face. At last I'd tracked down the dreaded Chain-Saw Fosworth, Queen of the Missing Rubbers.

The next second I'd lobbed a couple of smoke grenades through the glass of the door. Before Fosworth knew what had hit her I was in the room, the heat-seeking missile aimed straight at her earlobes.

'OK, Chain-Saw!' I barked. 'Hand over the rubber!'

Bam! The next second her metal-covered fist smashed into my nose and her knee came up into my guts. I hit the floor, at the same time grabbing for the machine-gun that I'd dropped. Her shoe came down hard on my fingers. She stood there, glaring down at me as I spat blood . . .

* * *

'Get back to your desk, Potts,' she snapped.

'Yes, Miss Fosworth,' I said.

CHAPTER EIGHT

Sir Edward Potts – Actor

'Potts,' said Mr Clench the drama teacher, 'you're going to be in the school play.'

Wow! This is it! At last, my new career – I am going to be an actor! As I wandered home after school for tea, I surveyed my new career. The wonder! The glory! The deserved acclaim . . .

* * *

'And the Oscar for Best Actor goes to . . . Edward Potts!'

I walked up on the stage to receive my Oscar, and turned to smile at the audience full of cheering film stars, all applauding in recognition of my tremendous acting talent.

'Thank you, thank you,' I said. 'Although I have won this Oscar, there are many people I would like to thank for my success: including the producer of this great film, whose name for the moment escapes me. Also I mustn't forget the writer and the director, although, as most people know, I rewrote most of the script myself and also took over the direction. I also found it necessary to re-design most of the costumes. I also worked the camera with a piece of elastic tied to my left shoe for all the scenes that I was in. However, I am only a humble actor and for that reason I can understand why I have only been awarded the Oscar for Best Actor.

'Before I go there are just a few people I would like to say hello to.'

And with that I opened the Hollywood Phone Book and began to read: 'A1 Investigations; Aardvaark Assurance Company; Abrahams, M; . . . ' Six hours later I finished with: 'Zanowski, Vera.' With that I stepped down from the stage to ecstatic applause and rushed off in my solid gold limousine to the TV studios where I was to be interviewed before a celebrity audience.

'Sir Edward,' said the TV host, 'it must have been a real honour for you to get a knighthood. How old were you exactly when you became Sir Edward Potts?'

'Let me see,' I said, 'I think I was . . . fourteen.'

'And you're sixteen now and you've already played every great part both in the theatre and in films: Macbeth, King Kong, James Bond, Superman . . . '

'True,' I said.

'Is there any particular part you haven't played that you wish you had?'

'Yes,' I said. 'As an immensely famous and talented classical actor it saddens me that I never got the chance to take on one of the truly great roles. I am referring, of course, to Freddy Kruger in *Nightmare on Elm Street*. I have a glove just like the one he wears, except instead of blades on the fingers I have lollipop sticks, but apart from that it looks just like it.'

FANTASTIC PICTURES PRESENT
SIR EDWARD POTTS AS FERDY IN
NIGHTMARE AT BEECHWOOD HIGH SCHOOL

The film opens in a graveyard at midnight. A vampire comes home after a hard night's work sucking the blood out of a family who live in an old castle at the end of the street. This has been a tough job of work for him because, owing to too much fluoride, he has lost all his teeth and can't get a decent grip on their necks with his gums.

A werewolf comes lumbering in, stops and cocks its leg against a tree, before disappearing into the undergrowth to reappear a few minutes later as one Herbert Henderson, sometime Headmaster of Beechwood High School.

I poke my head up from a grave and take a look around me. A passing mummy screams, 'Aaargh! It's Ferdy! There's about to be another Nightmare!' and goes rushing off across the graveyard, his bandages trailing behind him in such a manner that he trips and goes bum over eyebrows straight down into a nearby cellar.

* * *

At this point Mum came into the living-room and turned off the video which I was watching while eating my tea.

'How can you watch frightening rubbish like that in this house?' she yelled. 'It is sick trash and I will get your father to tell you off when he gets home. Why don't you watch *this* instead?'

She took out my video and stuck in *Peter Pan*, which has a crocodile that wants to eat human beings, a man with a hook instead of a hand with which he slashes people, and little boys kidnapped and kept in forced labour deep under the ground. Huh! So much for not watching frightening videos.

For nights after, I was unable to sleep for fear that the alarm clock beside my bed would turn into a crocodile.

CHAPTER NINE

Potts – Lord of Atlantis

'Right, all swimmers at the deep end, First-Years and non-swimmers at the shallow end!'

The school was at the Pond Street Swimming Baths for our monthly swimming lessons, and once more I was suffering the humiliation of being sent to stand by the side of the pool with the First-Years and the oddballs and the weaklings, like Loony Moffatt and Derek Dandruff Nelson. In vain I protested to Mr Fitch, the swimming instructor, that I *can* swim, that swimming with one foot on the bottom in the shallow end *is* swimming and that one day this style would be recognized as such and would be featured in the Olympics . . .

* * *

' . . . And here we are in the Olympic Swimming Pool Stadium, and the contestants in the Swimming With One Foot On The Bottom Across The Shallow End are, for Great Britain, Edward Potts . . . '

* * *

'Get to the shallow end, Potts!'

Huh! I joined the three-centimetres-high First-Years and the idiots Loony and Dandruff, and stood there aloof, pretending to anyone watching that I was their instructor. This worked well until

Mr Fitch arrived and said, 'Right, everyone into the water!'

I was just standing there, wondering which bit was the warmest, when . . . SPLOSH!! and I was pushed in by an unseen hand. I immediately went into my Patented Underwater Dive . . .

* * *

Captain Memo navigated his submarine, the *Nautilus*, deep beneath the sea, seaching along the deepest bed of the ocean.

'Are you sure this is where the lost land of Atlantis was, Captain?' asked his whiskered old Second Mate, Dean.

'Absolutely certain,' answered Captain Memo. 'According to my charts, this is where, many thousands of years ago, there lived a race who were able to live underwater without using snorkels. They were incredible swimmers and it is said that they could swim as fast as the fastest fish.'

He broke off as he saw that Dean was staring in astonishment out of the porthole.

'Captain, look!' said Dean.

Captain Memo looked, and his mouth dropped open in astonishment. Surely it wasn't . . . it couldn't be . . . But it was! There, swimming towards them at the bottom of the ocean in that unmistakable swimming style of Atlantis (one foot on the bottom) was . . .

'What is it, Captain Memo?' asked Dean, astonished.

'It is one of the lost underwater men of Atlantis,' said Captain Memo.

Dean frowned.

'When you say "lost", does that mean he doesn't know where he is?'

'No, you idiot,' said Captain Memo. 'It means that I was right, this is where Atlantis was. Moreover, that swimmer is proof that Atlantis still exists!'

Meanwhile I, Potts, Lord of Atlantis, was swimming back to the city after a hard day's work on the fish farm, when I noticed the submarine on my port bow. Two men were peering out through a porthole at me. I recognized one of them from a photograph that I had seen in our daily newspaper, *The Atlantis Mirror*. Normally, it was full of stories about fish (e.g. 'Fish Robs River Bank'; 'Fish Scores Winning Goal for Cod XI in Final Against Atlantis', etc) but yesterday the headline had been: 'Captain Memo On His Way To Find Out If We Exist.'

This had caused much talk in Atlantis and we were all wondering what was the best thing to do. Some people thought it would be a good thing to let Captain Memo discover Atlantis and then we could all make a lot of money from the tourists who would come in. Others warned that if that happened then it would lead to loads of underwater submarines arriving, which would cause litter and pollution. Personally, I was on the side of the 'Keep Atlantis Secret' brigade. In my opinion, the last thing we wanted was publicity; we'd end up with zillions of visitors, which would cause traffic jams all over the sea and there'd be no place to swim without bumping into stalls selling Underwater Candy Floss and postcards of fish. And yet – Shock Horror! – here *I* was, giving away the existence of

Atlantis by being spotted by Captain Memo himself!

As I watched, a door in the side of the submarine opened and Captain Memo came out, clumping across the sea-bed towards me, wearing an old-fashioned diving suit. He had only gone a metre or so, when suddenly there was a movement in the sea above . . . and the next second a huge Great White Shark was heading towards the Captain, its mouth wide open and its razor-sharp teeth glinting in the light from the submarine!

I gave a hard shove with my foot on the sea-bed and swam swiftly towards the shark, reaching it just before its gaping mouth could grab Captain Memo. I gave the shark a hard right cross to the nose, then an uppercut with my left that snapped its jaws shut. Realizing it was beaten, the shark turned tail and fled.

I turned back to see if Captain Memo was all right, and saw, to my horror, that an octopus had appeared from under the sand of the sea-bed, had wrapped its tentacles around him and was even now squeezing him tighter and tighter, crushing him to jelly, drawing him nearer and nearer to its beak-like mouth.

With incredible agility, I leapt through the water and grabbed two of the octopus's tentacles and twisted them up behind its back.

'I give in!' squawked the octopus, and immediately it let Captain Memo go.

I released the octopus and watched it swim away as fast as its eight legs would carry it. Then I helped Captain Memo to his feet. As I watched, little bubbles came out of the glass bowl over his head, which was his diving helmet. In each bubble was a

word. I read the words as they bubbled out:
'You . . . saved . . . my . . . life . . . How . . .
can . . . I . . . ever . . . repay . . . you?'

From the pocket of my swimming trunks I pulled
out my waterproof notepad and my pen that writes
underwater, and wrote:

'By telling no one that you found us. Keep us as
your secret.'

Captain Memo read my note, and nodded. Then
he saluted, went back to his submarine, revved up
the engine and chugged off.

I watched him leave, a great feeling of relief
coming over me. I had saved Atlantis!

I stood for a moment, pondering over this, my
one foot on the sea-bed, when suddenly a raucous
voice cut through my happy thoughts . . . :

'Potts!'

'Yes, Mr Fitch?'

'What on earth are you doing standing there like
an idiot? This is a swimming session, you're supposed to be swimming – unless you're doing an
impression of a sinking brick, ha ha ha ha ha ha
ha. Now get across that bath . . . And take *both*
feet off the bottom!!'

I did as he said, and immediately sank and had
to be rescued by three tiny First-Years. See? I tried
to tell Mr Fitch, as he gave me artificial respiration
on the side of the pool. That's what happens when
you try to interfere with the natural swimming style
of a half-human half-fish person from Atlantis!

CHAPTER TEN

Captain Potts in Outer Space

'Today,' said Mr Whippis, our science teacher, 'we are going to look at the Solar System.'

This was, of course, nonsense, as everyone in the class knew. We were *not* going to look at it; we were going to have to learn loads of facts and figures and stuff about it. If we were really going to *look* at it, then we'd all go to the windows and look up into the sky. Personally, I thought this would be a much better idea and I was about to suggest this to Mr Whippis, stressing its educational value, when he glared at me.

'Shut up, Potts,' he growled.

Good Heavens! I thought. The man is telepathic! What other explanation could there be for the fact that he knew I was going to say something? All right, it *could* have been the fact that my mouth was open, but that is how I breathe.

'The planet Mercury is fifty-eight million kilometres, or thirty-six million miles, from the Sun.' said Mr Whippis, and immediately seven children at the back of the class fell asleep with boredom. 'The planet Venus is one hundred and eight point two million kilometres from the Sun, or sixty-seven point two million miles. The Planet Earth . . . '

Once again it occurred to me: why do teachers make really interesting things so boring? Where is the excitement? Where is the adventure? Where is the sense of wonder and danger? Where is Captain Potts and the Starship Beechwood . . . ?

* * *

'Warp factor six, Mr Zulu.'

'Warp factor six it is, Captain Potts.'

Star Date: 4657. Captain's Log: I am Captain of the Starship Beechwood and me and my crew are boldly going where no person has gone before . . . into The Unknown! Not a lot is known about The Unknown, which is why it is called The Unknown.

Lately there have been disturbing reports about violent space activity in the region of the Planet Klonk, which is right next door to The Unknown. Missiles and space whirlpools have been appearing suddenly out of nowhere and thudding into the Planet Klonk, causing the inhabitants of the planet great concern. It is suspected that there is a Terrible Being lurking in the vastness of The Unknown, preparing to attack and engulf our whole Universe, starting with the Planet Klonk . . .

Suddenly, over the intercom, came a shout from the Engine Room.

'Captain!' It was the voice of my faithful First Engineer, Dean Morrison, or 'Spotty' as he is known to his friends. (Actually he only has one friend, me, so everyone else just calls him Morrison.)

'What's up, Spotty?' I asked.

'We've got trouble here in the Engine Room. Number One engine is overheating, Number Two engine has lost a pedal, and the rubber band has just come off Number Three Engine.'

I quickly thought it over, then reached a decision.

'Switch everything to Number Four engine,' I commanded.

There was a pause, then Spotty said: 'We only have three engines, Captain.'

I nodded.

'Just testing,' I said. 'Okay, we'd better crank all three engines up as fast as they'll go, hit Warp Speed, and then we can at least glide at trillions of miles an hour when they pack up.'

'Right, Captain,' said Spotty.

'Do you think that's wise, Captain?' said a voice at my shoulder.

Good heavens! I thought. A talking shoulder!

I looked around. It was not my shoulder talking, it was the spaceship's brainiest big-head, Lieutenant Zog, my Second-in-Command from the Planet Kupp, whose people had invented the flying saucer.

'Why not?' I asked coldly. I was beginning to get fed up with this clever-clogs Lieutenant Zog, who always seemed to know better than everyone else.

'Because there is a serious and severe possibility factor that the excessive energy loading thus inflicted on our three energy generators could result in a significant adverse reaction, thus bringing about an unstable equilibrium.'

I looked at him blankly.

'Eh?' I said.

'I think he means they could all blow up, Captain,' said Lieutenant Winters.

'Precisely,' nodded Zog.

'Then why don't you say so,' I snorted. 'Anyway, that's nonsense, and I should know because I'm the Captain and it's my ship, so there.' Into the intercom I said, 'OK, Spotty, go to Warp Speed.'

'Aye aye, Captain,' said Spotty.

There was a WHOOOSHHH and we began to accelerate at incredible speed, and then suddenly there was a BANG! BOOM! BANG! as our three engines blew up.

The crew, including Lieutenant Zog, turned to look at me.

'Okay,' I said. 'Go to Plan B.'

'What's Plan B?' asked Lieutenant Winters.

'We drift helplessly in Space.'

And so we drifted helplessly in Space until, eventually, we reached the area around the Planet Klonk.

Star Date: 123456789. Captain's Log: We are drifting helplessly in a hovering position above the Planet Klonk. My plan B is working . . .

'All right, to your stations!' I commanded. 'Prepare to beam down.'

Once we were on the surface of the Planet Klonk my intention was to go from there into The Unknown and find out what was causing the major disturbance that was threatening the Universe.

'You're in charge of the ship while I'm gone, Lieutenant.' I told Zog. 'Don't break it.'

Then First Engineer Spotty Morrison and I stepped on to the Transporter Pad.

'Okay,' I said. 'Beam us down.'

There was a ZIZZZ and suddenly . . . AAARGHHHH! Our teleporting bodies had been grabbed by some mysterious force and were being dragged into the centre of The Unknown.

'Help, Captain, I am being sucked into this great big Black Hole!' yelled Spotty.

The next second . . . PWHTT!! and Spotty vanished, and I was alone, materializing inside a cage.

What was this?! I was trapped! But who had taken me a prisoner?

'So . . . !' cackled an evil voice from behind me.

I turned, and there, smirking evilly at me through the bars of the cage, was none other than that Villain of the Universe . . . Miss Fosworth! And behind her lurked her henchman, the incredibly stupid but violent Mugger Smith! Both of them were dressed in what appeared to be Monster Outfits, or maybe it was just that they had become uglier the nearer they got to the centre of The Unknown.

'At last, Captain Potts!' snarled Monster Fosworth. 'Now you and the Starship Beechwood are mine! Ha ha ha ha ha!!!'

'Ha ha ha ha ha!!' echoed the Monster Smith. 'Beg for mercy!'

Never! I would not let them defeat me. My lips curled in a brave smile as I stared back at them through the bars of the cage . . .

* * *

'What are you grinning at, Potts!' growled Mr Whippis. 'Do you find the fact that Uranus is 2,869,600,000 kilometres from the Sun *funny*? Perhaps you'd like to share the joke with us, and let me warn you that if it is anything to do with the word Uranus then you'll be sorry,' etc etc etc etc.

I sighed. All right. I was trapped by the incredibly ugly space demon Whippis for the moment, but I calculated that my time of captivity would only last another one minute and then . . .

* * *

DRINGGGG!!! the bell for break! Immediately

Captain Potts made his break for freedom . . .
but . . .

* * *

'Potts! Get back here! During break you will stay
in and list all the planets of the Solar System. You
too, Smith, since you think it's so funny!'

Oh well, back in the cage! I opened my Science
exercise book and took a quick look around the
classroom for possible ways of escape. The windows were shut tight and Mr Whippis was standing
on guard by the door. Behind me, Mugger Smith
was glaring at my back, already blaming me for
being kept in and planning ways to break every
bone in my body as soon as Mr Whippis turned his
back for just half a second. There was only one
way out of this terrible spot. I picked up my pencil
case, held it close to my mouth, opened my lips
and whispered:

'Beam me up, Zog.'

CHAPTER ELEVEN

Dr van Potts – Vampire Hunter

'If you turn to page seventy-two of your text books,' droned Mr Whippis, 'you will find a picture of the common or lesser bat, which is not to be confused with the rarer species of Vampire bat, which you will see pictured opposite on page seventy-three.'

'Sir,' asked Goofy Biggins. 'Is it true what they say about Vampire bats?'

'That depends on what they say about them, Biggins,' said Mr Whippis. 'If they say that they will win the Singles Championship at Wimbledon I think that highly unlikely, ho ho ho ho ho ho.' And then he gave that awful sort of laugh that teachers give when they have made a poor, innocent pupil look an idiot in front of the whole class.

'I meant about them sucking blood out of people.' said Goofy.

'That,' said Whippis, 'is a myth. Vampire bats only suck the blood from the hooves of cows. These poor creatures have been for too long the innocent victims of malicious propaganda against them. Turning again to page seventy-two . . . '

Morrison and I exchanged meaningful looks. Sucking blood from the hooves of cows! Hah! What rubbish! As if any decent vampire worth its weight was going to waste its time looking for a likely cow's hoof to sink its teeth into! For one thing, it would be in serious danger of getting trodden on and flattened! I ask you, when did anyone last see Dracula or any of his accomplices flapping around a cow-shed checking hooves out as a likely source of nourishment?

It also sounded highly suspicious to me the way Mr Whippis was defending these bats – all this 'these poor creatures have been for too long the innocent victims of malicious propaganda against them' stuff. To my mind, it meant only one thing . . . Mr Whippis, as I had suspected for some time, was actually a vampire himself!

Beneath the cover of my desk I sharpened my pencil, preparing a small wooden stake, just in case. I spent the rest of the lesson watching Mr Whippis closely, looking out for any tell-tale signs that he was about to turn into a vampire, such as his front teeth (which do look suspiciously as if they protrude) suddenly becoming pointed, and his arms turning into big black wings. We were lucky that outside the sun was shining and it was broad daylight, but it only needed a cloud to cross the sky and plunge our classroom into darkness, and then . . .

* * *

Through the rocky crags of Transylvania our coach rattled, until finally I called out:

'Stop!'

My assistant, Igor Dean Morrison, pulled the horses to a halt.

'What's up, Dr van Potts?' he asked. 'Have you got to go to the toilet again?'

'No,' I said. 'Look, there, ahead of us.'

We both looked and saw through the gathering gloom the menacing outline of Castle Beechwood, home of the dreaded Vampire Whippis family.

'There!' I said. 'Inside that hideous monstrosity we will confront our deadly enemy. Have you got the stake ready?'

'I'm afraid the butcher only had sausages, Dr van Potts . . .' began Morrison.

'Not *steak*, you idiot! *Stake*, as in long wooden pointed thing, for use in bashing through the hearts of vampires as they lie sleeping!'

'Oh, I'm sorry . . .'

'No matter,' I said. 'We still have the garlic.'

'What garlic?' asked Morrison.

'The garlic you bought at the grocers on the corner before we left.'

'Oh, I knew there was *something* I had to get!' said Morrison.

'You mean we haven't got the garlic either?' I cried, aghast. 'Then how are we to protect ourselves if night should suddenly fall?'

'It won't suddenly fall.' said Morison. 'It's eleven o'clock in the morning.'

At that moment there was an eclipse of the Sun, and the whole of the countryside was plunged into instant darkness.

'See?' I said.

'Gosh!' said Morrison, and I could see by the whites of his eyes that he was worried. 'What do we do now?'

'From here we walk,' I said. 'If we try to go any further in the coach in this darkness, the horses could stray off the road and we could end up in the river.'

'Right,' said Morrison.

We clambered down from the coach, stepped forward . . . and fell into the river. The splash was so loud that it frightened the horses and they galloped off back the way we had come, taking the coach with them.

'Great idea!' said Morrison, sarcastically, as we dragged ourselves out of the river.

'Water is a protection against vampires,' I reminded him.

With that we set off to walk with a splosh and a squelch on our way towards Castle Beechwood.

When we arrived the castle was in darkness. Only a few bats flapped their way around, nipping in and out of the windows. Obviously this place didn't have double-glazing.

Morrison looked up at the darkened castle.

'I don't think anyone's in,' he said. 'Maybe we'd better come back later.'

I looked at him, shocked.

'Morrison,' I said, accusingly. 'You're scared!'

'No I'm not!' he said. 'It's just that . . . well . . . it's cold and vampires can be dangerous creatures if you don't know how to handle them.'

'You forget,' I reminded him, 'I am Dr Edward van Potts, the famous vampire hunter. No harm can come to you while you're with me.'

With that I took hold of the large handle sticking out of the castle wall that said: 'DOORBELL. NO SALESMEN, POLITICIANS OR VAMPIRE HUNTERS. PULL TO RING.' I pulled. Almost at once a large drawbridge fell out from the castle and thudded down on Morrison, squashing him into the ground.

'Ouch!' he said.

I helped him out from under the drawbridge.

'I thought you said no harm would come to me while I'm with you?' he said.

'A minor accident,' I said. 'Follow me.'

We stepped across the threshold of the castle and listened. As we stood there I could hear an eerie knocking sound.

'Listen!' I said. 'I expect that's a vampire, knocking to come out of its coffin.'

'Wrong,' whispered Morrison. 'That's my knees knocking together.'

Suddenly we heard the awful sound of the flapping of wings, and then feet landing close beside us. We turned, and beheld the awful sight of Mr Whippis with his hideous teeth and his bloodshot eyes.

'He's been on the booze again,' said Morrison.

'No!' I said. 'Don't you understand, it's what I've always suspected! Mr Whippis is a vampire!'

'Ah-ha!' crowed the awful figure in front of us. 'But you shall not live to tell your story! One bite of your necks and you shall be my slaves!'

And with that he advanced upon us, his long black cloak trailing behind him.

Suddenly I realized what day it was! Easter day! Just the previous week my granny had given me one of her home-made hot cross buns as a present. With luck, I still had it on me. I reached into my coat pocket. There it was! Quickly, I pulled it out of my pocket and held it up before Whippis's eyes, aiming the cross straight at him.

'Now!' I said in triumph. 'Do your worst!'

Vampire Whippis sneered.

'You fool, Potts. Can't you see what has happened to the cross on your bun?'

I looked, and gasped in horror. As was typical of my granny's cooking, the bun's cross had come unstuck and fallen off in crumbs inside my pocket.

'Argh!' I yelled, and frantically searched around

for something else to use as a weapon against the deadly creature who was now coming towards me, flexing his fangs prior to sinking them into my neck.

'But first,' he crowed, 'I shall slake my hunger with a bite from this bun.'

And with that he snatched my granny's hot crossless bun from my trembling fingers and gulped it down. The next second he was writhing on the floor in agony, and then suddenly he disappeared in a puff of smoke, leaving only a pile of dust lying in the corridor.

'That'll teach him, Morrison,' I said. 'I've always said that my granny's cooking is too much for anything to stomach.'

CHAPTER TWELVE

The Great Pottsinski – Magician

I was standing in the playground, talking to my
friend Dean Morrison about a show that had been
on TV the night before where this magician had
sawn a woman in half, and we were saying what a
good idea and why didn't we try it on Miss Fosworth and did we think the Headmaster would
insist we stuck both halves back together again
afterwards, when Melanie Winters passed us, talking to her friend Mad Tompkins of 3C.

'Did you see that magician on telly last night,
Paul Shazam?' she was saying. 'Wasn't he great?!
Didn't he just make your legs go all weak? He
could make me vanish like that any time.'

I was just about to run after her and say, 'I saw
Paul Shazam! I saw Paul Shazam!' but unfortunately *my* legs went all funny and I went all weak
and I sagged back against the wall.

'What's the matter?' asked Dean. 'Are you going
to be sick? Only these are my best trainers.'

In my chest my passion raged. I had to reveal it
to someone, or I would burst.

'Can you keep a secret?' I asked him.

'Course,' said Dean.

'Cross your heart, finger across your throat, spit
three times and you'll be turned into the ugliest
toad ever if you ever tell?'

'Course,' said Dean, and he crossed his heat, ran
his finger across his throat, and spat three times,

81

the last two unfortunately landing right on my shirt front.

'There,' he said. 'Your secret will go with me to my grave.'

'Right,' I said. 'I'm in love.'

Dean looked after the two girls who had just passed us, one (Melanie) walking on air, and the other (Mad Tompkins) lurching along like something out of *Return of the Evil Dead*. He looked back at me and gaped.

'You don't mean . . . ?' he said.

I nodded. I had to admit it.

'Yes,' I said. 'It is true.'

'Ummagummawow!!' he shrieked. 'Potts is in love with Mad Tompkins!!'

The next second he was off across the playground, shouting out: 'Potts is in love with Mad Tompkins! Pots is in love with Mad Tompkins!'

All eyes immediately turned to look at me and I could feel my ears heating up to a temperature of one thousand degrees centigrade and curling up at the sides of my head. So much for secrecy! And how could he even begin to think that my love – so deep, so true – was for Mad Tompkins? Yurk!!

However, I now knew what fired passion in Melanie's heart. All I had to do was to learn how to turn a bowl of fruit into an elephant and she would fall swooning into my arms! That night when I got home from school – the shouts of the whole of 2F still ringing in my ears – 'Potts is in love with Mad Tompkins! Potts is in love with Mad Tompkins!' etc etc etc – I took my 'Uncle Wizzo's Complete Conjurer's Outfit' down from the top of my wardrobe, blew the dust off, then opened it up and set to work to turn a handkerchief into a ping-pong ball. Soon, Melanie Winters would return my love . . .

* * *

'Ladies and gentlemen, tonight, and tonight only, the Great Pottsinski will amaze and astonish you with his devastating and astoundingly enormous range of magic tricks and illusions, from tricks like turning a handkerchief into a ping-pong ball, to turning a ping-pong ball into a handkerchief! And many more! Ladies and gentlemen . . . The Great Pottsinski!'

Roll of drums and flash of lights and a cloud of purple smoke, and suddenly there I was, waving my magic wand and hurling thunderbolts around all over the place.

'Good evening,' I said. 'For my first trick I require the assistance of a member of the audience.'

'Me!' cried a familiar voice, and the next second Mugger Smith had clambered up on to the stage. 'I love magic tricks! What do I have to do?'

'Nothing,' I said. 'I am the magician, I do it all.'

Then . . . SHAZAM!! ZAP!! and with one wave of my magic wand I had transformed him into a frog. He hopped out of the hall, never to be seen again.

'For my next trick I shall require the help of the most beautiful girl in the whole wide world. How about you, young lady?'

'Oh, wow!' breathed Melanie Winters. 'The Great Pottsinski is pointing at me!!'

She stepped up on to the stage and I gave her one of my special smiles that made her go weak at the knees.

'If you will step into this box . . . ' I said.

Melanie Winters stepped in, and as she did so her lips brushed against my cheek.

'You are so wonderful, Mr Pottsinski,' she whispered.

'I know,' I said. 'And you can call me "Great". What about a pizza after the show and then back to my place to watch *Nightmare on Elm Street* on video?'

'Oh, wow!' she said, and she stepped into the box.

'And now!' I announced to the audience, 'I will perform the most spectacular trick invented in the whole history of magic! I will make this girl disappear and then materialize at the bus-stop outside this theatre!'

There were gasps of admiration from the audience as I waved my magic wand over the box. 'Hocus pocus woo woo woo!' I chanted. And then I threw open the box to reveal that it was empty!

Unfortunately it wasn't. Instead, out stepped the glowering figure of Mad Tompkins of 3C.

'What do you mean by going around telling everyone that you're in love with me!' she yelled.

Before I had a change either to: a) explain; or b) duck, she belted me one in the eye.

'Make that disappear, Great Pottsinski!' she snarled.

And with that she stormed off.

'Fraud!' yelled the audience, while from the back of the theatre came the voice of Melanie Winters shouting: 'So you're in love with my best friend! You two-timing rat!'

And with that she chucked an ice-cream at me and left.

I did the only thing I could under the circumstances: I vanished.

CHAPTER THIRTEEN

Eddy Kool – Rock Star

'This is a sea shanty,' said Mr Barnstaple, our music teacher. 'You will all enjoy this.' With that he proceeded to bash the living daylights out of the keys of the school piano and started to sing some incredibly long song that seemed to consist mostly of 'Hey-Ho Heave-Ho'. What on earth gave him the idea that anyone with even fifty per cent hearing was going to enjoy it was beyond me.

'Now,' he said, when he was finished, 'I am going to play it again and you will join in at the chorus.' Then . . . KerPLUNK KerPLUNK THWONK!

> Hey ho heave-ho
> Hey ho heave-ho
> Hey ho heave-ho
> Hey ho heave-ho
> etc etc etc

As I joined in with all this 'hey-hoing' (or pretended to. Like everyone else I was just opening and closing my mouth to give the impression that I was singing. Luckily for all of us, Mr Barnstaple was too wrapped up in his own singing and playing to notice that the only voice warbling away was *his*, while we all stood there opening and closing our mouths in time to the piano like a row of goldfish.) As I say, while I was 'hey-hoing' it occurred to me, not for the first time, that music teachers at school have no idea of what music is really about. How can we expect to all become Major Rock Stars and appear on *Top of the Pops* if all we ever learn is this 'Hey-ho' stuff . . . ?

* * *

FAN MAGAZINE STAR INTERVIEW
THIS WEEK: EDDY KOOL!!

Eddy Kool is a phenomenon in the world of rock 'n roll. This teenage superstar was catapulted to overnight fame after his debut single, Eddy Kool Is Brilliant *went quadruple platinum all over the globe, hitting the Number One spot in every country of the world.*

Our reporter, Melanie Winters, went to inverview Eddy at the huge mansion he has built next to Buckingham Palace in the centre of London . . .

* * *

The first thing you notice about Eddy is that he is handsome and tall. This is unusual in the world of rock, where most rock stars are so short they could shelter from rain under a mushroom and not have to bend over to do it.

Eddy welcomed me to his mansion with a smile that made my heart skip a beat.

'Hi,' he said, 'You're Melanie Winters from Fan Magazine. *You don't know me but I'm Eddy Kool.'*

And with that he took me by the hand and led me into his home. His grip was firm and yet at the same time gentle, and not for the first time a voice inside me said, 'Wow! I'm in love!'

There is only one word to describe Eddy's mansion: fantabulisticowowist!

The man has incredibly brilliant artistic taste. One wall is decorated with great and original oil paint-

ings: The Mona Lisa *by Leonardo da Vinci, Van Gogh's* Sunflowers, *and the one where a queue of dogs in funny clothes are lining up to pee against a tree.*

I looked into that handsome face and for a moment I just wanted to throw myself at him and holler 'Eddy Kool, I love you! Take me!' But duty called. I switched on my Fan Magazine *portable cassette recorder (available from* Fan Magazine *at the Special Offer price of £179.99 (plus postage and packing) and began:*

Q: Eddy, you've had ten Number One records both here and in the USA. You've earned billions of dollars. Has this success changed you in any way?

A: No, I don't think so. I'm still the same handsome and incredibly talented person that I always was, but now my talent has been recognized by the world. So I suppose you could say that the world has changed in its attitude towards me, not me in my attitude towards the world.

Q: Wow, you're such an intellectual!

A: I know. I think the days when rock stars were seen as morons with hardly two words to rub together has gone.

Q: There are rumours that you are running for Prime Minister. What do you say to that?

A: The same as the rumours about me running for anything. I think exercise is bad for you.

Q: Can we talk about the new album . . . ?

A: Why not.

Q: This time you've written all the songs on the album . . .

A: I also play every instrument on the record, and I produced it. And I also designed my album sleeve. I wanted this to be my *statement of simplicity.*

Q: It's called Eddy Kool – First Genius of Rock.

A: Yes, I believe I have to be fair and honest to my fans. They expect it of me.

Q: And I understand you're planning a tour to go with the album.

A: Yes, I haven't been on the road for almost two weeks and my fans are starting to get withdrawal symptoms. I can understand that. So, out of love for my fans, I'm embarking on a major tour lasting one year, covering the whole wide world, and I'll be appearing in seven hundred and thirty different cities.

Q: That's two cities a day!

A: That's right.

Q: Won't you find it exhausting.

A: I hope not. The main problem is going to be transporting and constructing the set at each venue. We have this amazing set consisting of four hundred life-size inflatable elephants which float out into the arena across the audience; a three-hundred piece band and orchestra to recreate the sound that I achieved in the studio for the album; and a huge flying saucer one kilometre across that lands on stage at the climax of the show.

Q: Wow! Spectacular! But the planning of such a mammoth world tour as this must have caused you major organizational headaches?

A: Only one, really . . .

Q: Oh? What's that?

A: Making sure I get fresh cornflakes for breakfast every morning. That could have presented a difficulty in the middle of the Amazon jungle, but fortunately the RAF have arranged to fly some in for me.

Q: Getting back to the music, would you like to play a song for us from the album?

91

A: Yes. This is the third track on the A side, and it's also the new single.
Q: What's it called?
A: It's based on old sea-shanty that I once heard. It's called Hey-Ho, *and it goes like this:*

> *Hey ho heave-ho*
> *Hey ho heave-ho*
> *Hey ho heave-ho*
> *Hey ho heave-ho . . .*

'Potts!'

'Yes, Mr Barnstaple?'

'Your singing is atrocious. From now on, just open and close your mouth and *pretend* to sing, like all the other rotten singers in the class. Right, everyone, after three. One – two – three . . .

> Hey ho heave-ho
> Hey ho heave-ho
> Hey ho heave-ho
> Hey ho heave-ho

CHAPTER FOURTEEN

Edward Potts – Green Hero

'And as a result of this excess of carbon dioxide, we get the Greenhouse Effect, which means that the planet is heating up and, unless something is done about it, our planet as we know it will overheat and eventually shrivel up into a lump of uninhabitable hot dust floating in space.'

With that the bloke who had come in to talk to us from Friends of the Earth gave us all a smile and sat down. We all sat agog and in shock as Miss Fosworth got to her feet. At least, I sat there all agog and in shock, the rest of 2F did what they normally do on occasions like this, which is pull faces at each other and pick their noses.

'Thank you, Mr Porridge,' said Miss Fosworth, 'for a most enlightening talk.'

Enlightening?! Ths world is about to turn into a crisp and this woman calls it enlightening! 'Terrifying' I would have thought was a more suitable word.

At break I walked over to my friend Dean Morrison, who was blowing bubbles from one of those little soap things with a stick with a hole in it, and pointed out to him that every time he blows a bubble it sends carbon dioxide up into the atmosphere and destroys the Ozone Layer (or something else that's up there).

Dean looked at his bubble maker.

'Wow!' he said. Then he looked across the playground. 'Look, there's Mugger Smith using one,' he said. 'Hadn't you better go and tell him about it as well?'

I weighed this up, and decided that one act of 'green' heroism was enough for today. I would deal with Mugger Smith in a more subtle manner: I would make an anonymous phone call to the Ministry of the Environment and tell them what Mugger Smith was up to and suggest they lock him up for a hundred years.

My first 'green' duty done, I then walked across the playground to tell off the tiniest First-Year in the school for dropping a crisp packet on the ground . . .

* * *

'Mr President! We've got a terrible problem!'

'What is it, Buck?'

'Our scientists report that the planet Earth as we know it is in a terrible state and it's going to end in ten years unless something is done to solve the pollution problem!'

'Ten years?! Oh no! What can we do?!'

'There's only one thing we can do, Mr President. Send for the Green Hero . . . Edward Potts!!'

WOW!! ZAP!! POW!!! The Green Hero, Edward Potts, stepped off his eco-friendly bicycle and strode into The White House.

'You sent for me, Mr President?'

'Yes, Potts. You know the problem?'

'I do indeed. Acid rain, destruction of the rain forests, polluted seas killing all marine life forms, radiation fall-out making all vegetation unsafe to eat and all water unsafe to drink, food contaminated with pesticides and chemical pollutants making all food on the planet deadly poisonous, global warming causing the seas to rise so that all land areas will be flooded. And that's just *half* the problem.'

The President thought this over.

'As bad as that, eh, Green Hero?'

'I'm afraid so, sir.'

'Then what can we do to stop the planet falling apart and becoming a lifeless heap of hot water?'

'There is only one answer.'

'What's that?'

'Lock up one Mugger Smith of Beechwood High School, Luton, Bedfordshire, England in a deep dungeon. And while you're at it, lock up his accomplices: one Chain-Saw Fosworth, Potty Clench, and anyone else walking around this same Beechwood High School pretending to be a teacher.'

'What good will that do?'

'It will stop me being bashed up and kept in all the time, and then I can get on with my proper job of Saving The Planet'.

'Leave it to me, Green Hero. Your wish is my command.'

And with that Mugger Smith and all my assorted enemies (including Spot the dog from next door) were rounded up and taken off in chains inside a fleet of armoured cars, and I could get on with stopping the world from being destroyed by pollution . . .

* * *

I began with that tiniest First-Year who had just dropped a crisp packet on the playground.

'Do you realize that by dropping that crisp packet

you are contributing to the litter mountains that add up to ten billion tonnes of litter per person per year and is causing plagues of rats and is choking this planet and causing us all to stop breathing? What are you going to do about it?'

'Push off, fish-face,' snarled the First-Year, who then stamped on my foot and ran off.

As I limped back into school I decided that I'd leave saving the planet until tomorrow.

CHAPTER FIFTEEN

Edward Potts – Time Traveller

I was sitting in class doing something called a Mock History Exam (which seriously seemed to resemble a Real History Exam because we all had to keep dead quiet while we did it, and if anyone so much as made a noise or dropped dead with a moan and a thud, they would be kicked out of the classroom). Anyway, as I sat there, I had to admit to being a bit baffled. It wasn't so much the *questions* I was having trouble with as the *instructions*, particularly this one: ALL CANDIDATES MUST WRITE ON ONE SIDE OF THE PAPER ONLY.

Obviously, Miss Fosworth had dug these exam papers from the Pyramids while out digging up mummies and things because they appeared Dead Ancient. For one thing, what is a 'candidate'? I thought they were the people who went in for elections to try to get into Parliament and stuff. Did they have to take these in order to get in? If so, how did they select them? From what I've seen of MPs, I reckon they choose the thick ones who can't answer anything. I let out a (silent) groan: if I ran true to form and got zero out of a hundred, *I'd* end up as an MP in Parliament! No, I had to write something down and get some marks, even if it was only for spelling my name correctly (I got it wrong the last test I took). But there was still this problem of the weird instruction about WRITE ON ONE SIDE OF THE PAPER ONLY. Oh well, I supposed they must know what they want. I looked at the first question: What important historical event happened in 1066 and what was the result? I wrote:

In
1066
England
won
the
World
Cup.
The
result
was
four
goals
to
two.

Frankly, this all seemed a bit crackpot to me. Here we were, worried about the disappearing forests, and these exam people were making us waste paper like this at a cost of billions of trees! Maybe I ought to get into Parliament after all, I thought, and stop this sort of thing happening. Who knows, I might even get to be Prime Minister and then I could really sort this world out . . .

* * *

MY ELECTION MANIFESTO

Vote for me coz I'm brilliant and if I was Prime Minister wars would be banned, everyone would have all the money they ever wanted and they'd only have to work if they wanted to. No one would starve or get ill coz all germs would be banned from entering the atmosphere of Planet Earth (except for germs that are good for you, like the ones Mr

Whippis our science teacher says turn milk into yoghurt). All schools would be shut and turned into multi-screen cinemas, and no one would be made to kiss their grandparents ever again!

Vote for me and get:
– Good weather
– Money
– Health
– To appear on TV and be famous
– Everything you ever wanted

* * *

Anyway, back to the history test. It occurred to me as I was halfway through writing my answer to Question Two: ('Write about three English Kings.')

King
Fred
I.
King
Fred
II.
King
Fred
III.
I
believe
I
am
right
about
them.

– it ocurred to me that the best thing for answering any history exam would be a Time Machine. Then you could zap backwards in time and find out the answers, and once you'd got them you could Fast Forward to one minute before the exam actually started! Brilliant . . .

* * *

ZAP! POW! SHAZAM!! Time Traveller EDWARD POTTS stepped into his Time Machine, pressed loads of buttons and made impressive looking numbers come up on a display panel. Then . . . WOOOOOOOOOOOOOOOSHHHHHHH!!!!!!! . . .

I stepped out of my Time Machine straight into the path of a charging lion. I was just about to punch it on the nose (but not too hard because I am kind to animals) when a gladiator threw a net over it.

'Thanks,' I said, and offered him a mint.

The next second, hordes of Roman soldiers (known as Centurions because they all look about a hundred years old) rushed into the arena, grabbed me and hauled me before a bloke dressed in a white sheet and with what looked like a haircut made of leaves. This was the Emperor Nero.

'Hi,' I said.

'Who are you, infidel, and by what right do you disturb our entertainment?' said Nero, looking angry. 'We are in extra time of the Semi-Final of the Roman World Cup with the score at Gladiators: 2; Lions: 2, and you dare to interrupt the game! You'd better have a good reason or else you will die!'

'I have a very important reason,' I said, and produced the Mock History Exam paper. 'In what year do you cause the destruction of the Roman Empire and die?'

103

'68,' said Nero.

'BC or AD?' I asked.

'Er . . . AD,' said Nero.

'Ta,' I said, and ticked that one off on my question sheet. 'OK,' I said, 'carry on.'

Then, before any of them could touch me I stamped on the nearest Centurion's foot (but gently, because he was a hundred years old), and then ran back into the arena, dodging a dozen heavily-armed gladiators as I did so. I reached my Time Machine, jumped in, pushed every button in sight and then . . . POW ZAP SHAZAM ZOOOOOOOOOOOMMMMMMM!!!!!!!!!!!

I stepped out of my Time Machine and found myself on the deck of a ship crammed with people dressed in big black hats and with the words 'PURITANS – FIRST AMERICAN TOUR' on their T-shirts.

'What year is this?' I asked one of them.

Unfortunately, he was Dutch and so he didn't understand my question.

Luckily for me, another Puritan, who happened to be passing, exclaimed suddenly: 'Mein Gott, what is that Time Machine doing on the deck of this good ship *Mayflower* on its way to America in this year of 1620?'

'Ta,' I said, and ticked off another question. Then once more back into my Time Machine and . . . POW ZAP SHAZAM ZOO-OOOOOOOOMMMMMMM!!!!!!!!!!!

The next time I stepped out of my Time Machine it was at the time of the Industrial Revolution and I was right in the middle of it! All around me machines were fighting with each other and chucking smoke and dust and soot at the nearest factory!

A large bulldozer came charging past me, intent on making a full forward attack on a line of human beings! A coal mine suddenly pulled itself up out of the ground and threw itself on a nearby city! What would happen next? Who was there whom I could ask about Question Four: 'Why did the Industrial Revolution happen and what were the consequences of it?'

As a factory chimney came lumbering towards me I got back into my Time Machine and headed back to the Mock Exam. When I got back I wrote down:

The
Industrial
Revolution
happened
because
the
machines
got
fed
up
with
being
treated
like
slaves.
The
machines
won.

There! All the right answers the easy way!

* * *

Next day when I saw Miss Fosworth in the corridor I gave her a smile and waited for her to rush up and shake me by the hand and give me her con-gratulations on getting A++++ and 150% in the Mock History Exam. She gave me a funny look. Shock, I suppose, at me knowing so much history.

'Potts,' she said.

'Yes, Miss Fosworth?' I said with a smile.

'You have the brain of a paralysed chicken.'

And with that she went.

Ah well, it just goes to show that some people have no appreciation of *true* history; they prefer to believe the rubbish that has been handed down through the ages by people who made it up because they didn't know the real facts. Huh!

CHAPTER SIXTEEN

Potts – World Sporting Champion

'And with just ten second to go the score here at Wembley Stadium is still England: 1, the Rest of the World: 1. But here comes Potts! He traps the ball neatly with his left knee, brings it down to his left foot, then goes past one man, two men, three men (went to mow, went to mow a meadow), four men . . . the whole Rest of the World team . . . there's just the goalkeeper, the giant four-metre-tall German, Willi Makeit, to beat . . . Potts shoots . . . and it's there! One of the most brilliant goals ever scored . . . possibly THE most brilliant! England: 2, the Rest of the World: 1 . . . And there's the final whistle, and England are the new Champions of the Universe! Thanks to wonderful Eddy Potts!'

'Here we are at the Centre Court in Wimbledon for the Final of the Men's Singles, where the Champion Bjorn Agane is playing England's Ed Potts. Potts is at a bit of a disadvantage, having just arrived hot foot from scoring the winning goal in the England versus the Rest of the World football match at Wembley, which ended just thirty minutes ago. I dread to think what would have happened if that game had gone into extra time: Potts wouldn't have been able to get to Wimbledon in time to play Agane and would have forfeited the Final. As it is, Potts was lucky that he had his own private helicop-

ter waiting at Wembley to bring him straight here.'
'It's first serve to Potts . . . and it's an Ace! Fifteen-
love to Potts . . . And another! And another!
Game to Potts . . .'

* * *

'Here we are at Melbourne for the Second Test,
with Australia leading England by two hundred
runs, and play has temporarily stopped as a helicop-
ter lands on the pitch, and out steps Edward Potts.
This boy is remarkable. To look at him you
wouldn't think that it was only a few hours ago that
he stepped off the Centre Court at Wimbledon in
England having just won the Men's Singles Championship after spectacularly defeating the Swede
Bjorn Agane, in three sets, six-love, six-love, six-
love. And this was just after scoring the winning
goal for England at Wembley in their match against
the Rest of the World.'
'Potts has just finished strapping on his pads and
he strides towards the crease with that unusual but
familiar stance that we in cricket know so well.
Hudson, the Australian bowler, goes back half a
mile; this is going to be a really fast one. Here
comes Hudson now, tearing towards the stumps,
going about two hundred miles an hour. He bowls
. . . and Potts smacks it straight out of the stadium
for two sixes and three fours and the crowd goes
mad! . . . And the Australian captain has declared!
The Australians know they can't win against Potts!
And England have won the Ashes!'

* * *

'And here we are in the last part of the Decathlon
at the Olympic Stadium here in Mexico City, and

110

the news is that thirty times' Gold Medallist, Edward Potts, who arrived here this afternoon straight from winning the Ashes for England in the Test against Australia in Melbourne . . .'

* * *

'Potts!'

'Yes, Miss Fosworth?'

'Stop gawping out of that window like an idiot and pay attention! Right, Class 2F, the list for who will be taking part in which event for our class in the School Sports. Potts.'

'Yes, Miss Fosworth?'

'You will be Third Reserve in the Egg and Spoon Race.'

'Yes, Miss Fosworth.'

CHAPTER SEVENTEEN

E.P. Goes Home

'E.P. go home . . . E.P. go home . . . '

It was Friday afternoon. The unhappy little creature from another planet looked at the clock hanging on the wall behind Miss Fosworth. How often
he had wished it had been Miss Fosworth hanging
on the wall instead. As the poor frail creature
watched, the big hand ticked slowly round,
until . . .

3.40pm! The shrill sound of the bell for the end of
school.

Wow! I yelled (silently). 'Jailbreak! Jailbreak!'
went up the cry all around me, and then everyone
was making a break for the door and two whole
days of freedom.

I hit the street, running. Goodbye, Beechwood
High School. Goodbye, Miss Fosworth. Goodbye,
Mugger Smith. And then there was the sound of a
thud as my heart broke as I thought . . . Goodbye,
Melanie Winters.

Then a Nice Thought sprang into my brain: it's
chips and baked beans for tea! With apple cake to
follow!

Instantly my broken heart mended. Life must go
on!

Intrepidly I turned and walked towards the sinking sun.

E.P. was going home.